A DARK DARK TALE

For William, Edward and Alice Cowling

First published in the United States 1981 by
Dial Books for Young Readers
A Division of NAL Penguin Inc.
2 Park Avenue, New York, New York 10016
Copyright © 1981 by Ruth Brown
First published in Great Britain
by Andersen Press Ltd.
Printed in Hong Kong by South China Printing Co.
COBE
10 9 8

Library of Congress Cataloging in Publication Data
Brown, Ruth. A dark dark tale.
Summary: Journeying through a dark, dark house,
a black cat surprises the only inhabitant
of the abandoned residence.
[1. Dwellings—Fiction. 2. Cats—Fiction.
3. Mice—Fiction.] I. Title. II. Series.
PZ7.B81698Dar 1981 [E] 81-66798
ISBN 0-8037-1672-9 AACR2
ISBN 0-8037-1673-7 (lib. bdg.)

The art consists of acrylic paintings that are
color-separated and reproduced in full color.

A DARK DARK TALE

Story and pictures by

RUTH BROWN

Dial Books For Young Readers / New York

Once upon a time there
was a dark, dark moor.

**On the moor there was
a dark, dark wood.**

In the wood there was
a dark, dark house.

At the front of the house
there was a dark, dark door.

40

Behind the door there
was a dark, dark hall.

In the hall there were
some dark, dark stairs.

Up the stairs there was
a dark, dark passage.

Across the passage was
a dark, dark curtain.

75

**Behind the curtain was
a dark, dark room.**

In the room was a dark,
dark cupboard.

In the cupboard was
a dark, dark corner.

In the corner was
a dark, dark box.

107

And in the box there was... A MOUSE!